# FLATLANDERS

## Short Fiction from Vermont

# FLATLANDERS

## Short Fiction from Vermont

Kathryn Holzman

# Table of Contents

# HOW TO SHARE A BLACKBERRY PATCH WITH A BLACK BEAR

1)  Don't be afraid to make noise. For once in your life, stomp your feet. Talk to yourself, sing. Talk to the bear, preferably before seeing her. Make it clear you will share the summer bounty and intend to leave the fruit just beyond your reach. Demonstrate your generosity by dropping a few berries among the robins who skitter in the fallen leaves around your feet. As you pick your way down your neighbor's grassy path, eyes peeled for berried branches, remind the bear that your reach is limited. Your wrists are already streaked red from the thorns that attack you as you reach on tippy toe for the fruit. Given the prevalence of poison ivy, surrender the innermost territory of the patch to your competition. The bear is bigger than you and, despite her reclusive nature, she will always win in a fight. Given this disparity in size and strength, never forget: the bear makes the rules.

2) This is a limited engagement. From the morning in early August when the green berries first blush red until the last soft blackberry plops to the ground just before the leaves burst into fall brilliance, the two of you share this territory in a temporary truce. Let the bear know you appreciate

the importance of wild berries to her survival, but remind her there are plenty to go around. Just as she must pack away the pounds before her winter hibernation, you are counting on your frozen harvest to sweeten the snowy months of cereal ahead.

3) Show some respect. Never come between a mother and her cub. Never ignore the snap of a twig in the lower field or the steady crackle of heavy footsteps approaching. Be on the alert. Bottom line: you are the visitor here and should graciously abandon your search if your host decides that this bright morning is ideal for foraging.

4) Don't let fear defeat you. The hemlock and pine forest surrounding the field where you stand is riddled with shadows. Chipmunks and squirrels scurry in the undergrowth, filling their larders. Blue jays squawk like chalk on a blackboard, competing with the crows for territory. Hummingbirds buzz in a frantic search for open lily blossoms. Like you, the surrounding creatures are going about their business. The raccoons and foxes will lie low until you finish. Go ahead, pick without populating the shadows with your febrile imagination. Only the resident bear should concern you.

5) Or perhaps the slam of your neighbor's car door. Your neighbor, unable to get clear reception of his satellite TV, cleared his wooded property of trees several years ago. Day after day, he sawed

away at towering pines until they came crashing down just short of your property line. He felled maple trees, piling their branches in large mounds, which he burned in smoky bonfires. His backyard transformed into a barren wasteland of lifeless timber, with trees sprawled out like corpses. In their wake, these wild berry bushes claimed the territory. Unlike the scrawny, leggy plants hidden by ferns and diminished by the canopy on your own lot, his berry bushes grow tall and heavy with fruit, nurtured by the composting wood and unobstructed sunlight in the devastated yard. You can feel the sunshine now in the swelling ripeness of the fruit you pick. Berries that double in size from one day to the next.

6) Consider this harvest a consolation prize, compensation for the gaping hole in the forest, the mess you overlook while sipping tea on your back deck. Your neighbor has shown no interest in the berry bushes which now flourish in his backyard in place of his view of the distant Green Mountains. So, pick on the mornings you see his station wagon back out of the driveway and turn toward the highway. Although your daily collection of ripe fruit might be construed by others as loot pilfered while trespassing, consider this an act of worship, appreciate nature's resiliency despite the destructive onslaught of humans concerned only with their own safety and security, and, apparently, unobstructed satellite TV reception.

7) You and the bear live off the earth. In synch. This is how you share a blackberry patch with a black bear. As you fill your basket, lift the canes to discover hidden clusters of ripe berries. It is quite possible the bear is watching from a distance, awaiting her turn, demonstrating the same respect you have shown her. If, oblivious to her presence, you walk too close, she will probably turn tail and disappear into the forest, more afraid of you than you are of her. In all likelihood, you have nothing to worry about.

8) Carry a whistle, just in case.

9) Your neighbor won't be home for hours. Think of this as a nonviolent demonstration of cooperation among predators. A restoration. A subversive reinstitution of the natural order.

10) After a storm, watch your footing. Don't sacrifice your position by falling on your face. Don't lose what you have collected with such deliberation. You don't want to look up and see a looming shadow. When you meet your neighbor at the post office, be polite. Discuss the weather.

11) A little cortisone cream on the rash erupting on your wrist will stop the itching. Think of the colander in the sink, cold well water running off the ripe berries, containers ready for freezing. Imagine the sweet taste of blackberries in the dead of winter. The bear asleep in her den, having survived another

hunting season without incident, her belly pregnant with masticated berries.

# SURFACING

They were married in the summer. The Justice of the Peace sat at the helm of the rowboat. From the shore, stereo speakers played the Wedding March. Renee wore a bathing suit and a veil and promised, for the second time in her life, to love another until death parted them.

Her regret wasn't that Stan asked her to marry him. She just wished he had not done so while telling her the story of the Harvard student who drowned in the pond after taking LSD. The bad timing was typical of Stan, a psychology professor incapable of distinguishing between joy and the macabre. Ultimately, her acceptance of his proposal reflected more on Renee who, raised by artists, was incapable of expecting a more conventional proposal. Spring had arrived and emerging flowers were about to open, and she had waited long enough.

From the living room of the house they had shared for two years, there was a clear view of the pond. Renee's mood was often subject to the seasonal changes of the water. In the fall, the pond reflected the changing leaves, the reds, yellows, and oranges blazing in undulations reflected on the living room ceiling. Stan and Renee met in the fall;

neither was young nor inexperienced, but they were comfortable in a way they hadn't felt when young and in love. They met at the home of a colleague from the university, two singles among the couples, relieved at the ease with which they could talk. Stan taught evolutionary psychology and discussed the modular view of the mind. Renee easily grasped the concept—different sub-routines that compete to control one's decisions, the lack of a unified essence, the need to invent a story to explain away the inconsistencies.

Renee moved in with Stan in winter when the pond had grown gray and icy with the reflections of leaf-less trees and clouds. Each year, the cycles of ice and thaw were slightly different. That first winter, Renee watched the neighborhood dogs run out onto the ice, oblivious, even before the water froze solid. Renee stood paralyzed at the window, always fearful of an ominous crack, a frantic yelp. She imagined herself running out to rescue, but doubted she had the nerve. In reality, she would be more likely to watch the rescue, or the drowning, from the privacy of her home.

This was her home now, a project of the heart that Stan built during his bachelor years, each floorboard laid by hand. The night they met, Stan gave her a tour–hardly more than a twirl–around the boxy energy-efficient cottage, switching between the theories of psychology and the satisfactions of carpentry. While Renee admired the view of the pond, Stan detailed the benefits of passive solar heating and listed the construction's low impact building materials. Renee brought almost nothing from her disastrous marriage; when she moved into the house it remained uncluttered, noticeably new. She stored her parents' paintings, her only inheritance, in the hall closet, content to leave the white walls unsullied.

When spring arrived, light filled their bedroom. They gloried in spring sex, that annual reawakening of urges they feared they might have lost. On one of these reassuring April afternoons, Stan told her the story of the student who drowned.

"Four Harvard students were camping on the far side of the pond. Can you see that tall pine in the cove on the right? Families and vacationers from New Jersey surrounded the pond.

"According to the town constable who guarded the site for weeks—and recounted his version of the events to any of us who would listen—the four students had set up an illicit campsite ignoring the 'No Overnight Camping' sign.

"The young men decided to take a moonlight swim on LSD. The moon was full, and the boy who died was an athlete and able swimmer. Crossing the pond should not have been difficult. When the campers regrouped later around the fire and he had not yet returned, they didn't worry. Several hours passed before they notified the authorities. When they did, the police did a midnight patrol of the pond but found no sign of him. They figured it was a misunderstanding. He was probably drinking a beer in the local pub. What could they do in the dark?"

The small pond warmed up by June and offered a welcome respite from the July heat.

"The next morning, the search resumed. A police rescue boat joined the search party. Again, no trace of the swimmer. It was the talk of the town. By now we all knew, thanks to the constable's updates, that the swimmer had been 'on drugs' and camping in an illegal site.

"The town, with reservations, closed down the beach fearful that a child might find the lifeless body. At noon, a hiker spotted a sneaker near the beaver lodge. There was nothing to do but wait.

"From our window, I saw the boy's parents when they arrived later that afternoon, a weeping girlfriend in tow."

Renee looked over to the pond, imagining the frantic parents speaking with the self-important constable. She imagined the yellow police tape and the many eyes observing their incomprehension.

"The constable told them what he had told us. If their son had drowned, the body would inevitably rise when the gases of decomposition built up. The body would inflate and float to the surface. They would have to wait. By week's end, they would know if he had survived."

The locals discussed the incident at the post office, where they picked up their mail. A missing boy, the drugs, the moonlight swim, the prestige of the student's college and his athleticism were topics of the week's gossip. The local kids were pissed at losing a week's swimming during an uncomfortable, warm week in July. He should have known better, they all agreed.

"Did the body ever float to the surface?" Renee, still picturing the parents' vigil, studied the pond; she strained to see what lay below the surface. Because it was spring, decomposing leaves still floated on the top of the water, hiding the depth below. On a walk the previous evening, she and Stan had searched for frog eggs clustered near the shores in gelatinous masses, primed to burst with life as the lengthening days of sunlight warmed the water. On this, the spring equinox, the pond teemed with new life, not death. Easier to imagine the student's psychedelic swim than his lifeless body swelling on the water's floor.

The summer pond water must have been warm and enveloping the night the student dived in. The full moon would have served as a beacon. An athlete, the swimmer would have been unafraid of exploring his hallucinations, surrounded by friends, with nature at its mildest. She thought of him looking up through the water's prism at the moon. The distortions of the water would have mimicked the drug's effects. She could almost see him floating there, embraced by the warm waves, lulled into a sense of safety as strangeness overtook him.

The same full moon had illuminated the night sky when Stan and Renee had taken a walk the previous evening. Holding hands, they discussed the many myths that marked the vernal equinox. The Roman Attis, a god of ever-reviving vegetation, reborn each year and celebrated on Black Friday. The pagan Ishtar commemorating the resurrection of the Akkadian vegetation god Tammuz, believed to be the only begotten son of the moon-goddess and the sun-god. Even Easter, celebrated on the first Sunday after the first full moon after the vernal equinox, evolved from thousands of years of spring rites and celebrations.

Walking the path from the lake shore, they saw signs of rebirth all around them. Renee named the light green leaves breaking through the leaf cover, wintergreen, and rattlesnake plantain, a delicate orchid. She shared her knowledge of botany, a welcome relief after years of lonely study, reading books in the basement library among fresh-faced students, a divorcee trying to rebuild a life.

Relishing their exchange, they walked slowly despite the evening's chill.

Had the student responded to the pull of the moon? Did the hallucinations of his trip draw him under?

As Stan spoke, Rene imagined the pond through his eyes: the air murky with rainbow-hued grasses waving him on, leading him into the Underworld. In the murky depths, he spies Persephone, who waits for him naked on the floor of the dark pond. He swims to her away from the summer heat, away from chattering friends, following a beaver who beckons, speaking in a language that suddenly becomes clear, ancient, and melodic. Each stroke of his arms in the water leaves a trail of evanescence. Moon rays disappear from his sight. He descends to his destiny. He swims with tears flowing, filling the pond with longing, a man among the demons, feet bleeding into the decomposing, rich mud of the pond floor.

Did the weight of the water suck the boy in? Did he breathe in the pond water thinking it air and liberation? Did he know what was happening that summer night?

Does anyone ever know what is about to happen?

Stan was asleep when the student died. In this same bed where they had just made love.

With dread, Renee waited for Stan to complete his story. They lay on the bed, lit by the rays of the still weak, but strengthening, spring sun. She pulled the winter blankets up, feeling a chill from the prematurely opened bedroom window. Perhaps they were moving too fast.

"Renee, wait, I want to ask you something."

"No. First, tell me, did they ever find the body?" she asked, haunted by the picture of the parents waiting for the constable's call.

"Eventually, yes. It took longer than expected. When the body surfaced, the coroner concluded his sneaker had gotten stuck in a beaver's lodge, holding him under." Stan was matter of fact. It was an old story, an oddity that was part of the pond's lore. He had something else on his mind.

The student struggled to break free. Rene had often idled near the lodge in her kayak, hoping to spot the beaver at his labors. Once she saw the flap of his tail and the resulting ripples spreading out toward her. She paddled closer, but the beaver disappeared into deeper water.

"Oh." Renee wrapped the wool blanket tighter. She had hoped for a last-minute twist, a happy ending. A re-emergence of the student somewhere else, drinking with coeds in a bar. Laughing at the misguided search. A resurrection. An apology to his friends and parents, those who loved him and who had suffered.

Had the girlfriend mourned?

"Renee, look at me." She turned her head, not ready to change the subject. Stan ran his fingers through her hair, slowly bringing her chilled body back to life. His fingers traced her mouth and stroked her neck. She watched him as he kissed her. His gaze was steady and his body solid. He looked into her eyes without apology. She took a deep breath.

"Let's get married on the pond."

Saying "yes" was as close to resurrection as Rene could muster.

# A CONNECTICUT YANKEE AT THE WEST BROOK DUMP

The Yankee drives an SUV with Connecticut plates through the rusted gate of the West Brook Transfer Station, careful to avoid the muddy potholes and multiple piles of discarded metal. In the back of his vehicle, on meticulous WeatherTech mats, he has stored four plastic black bags of garbage.

"You could use a few signs here," he says to Bill, the town-appointed guardian of the dump.

"Signs?" Bill asks. "You want signs? Drive down my driveway. 'Course you might get shot."

Frank pulls over next to the dumpster.

Without missing a beat, Bill, a slender man of medium build with close-cropped salt and pepper hair and amused gray eyes, opens the back of Frank's car and lifts out the bags of trash. "I've put up a few warnings to any fool who drives down my road. The first says Private Property, the next says Keep Out. The final one says Trespassers Will Be Shot." Bill cackles when he describes the hand-lettered cardboard signs he has nailed to the pine trees along his drive.

Frank figures he's better off not asking questions. Maybe the signs protect Bill's extensive marijuana crop, or maybe the man enjoys intimidating intruders. It's hard to tell. Bill never lacks for a story. It is anyone's guess which ones can be believed.

After ten summers in the Green Mountains, Frank has learned the Vermont motto, *Freedom and Unity* might lack the bombastic glory of New Hampshire's declaration, *Live Free or Die*, but it captures the Vermont spirit of stubborn cooperation. He's heard this all before. Bill's declaration: "Nobody tells me what to do." Heaven help the man or woman who places household garbage in the recycling bin. To deter this sacrilege, Bill often greets residents as they pull their pickup trucks into the dump and offers to sort through their garbage bags. Bill lectures with righteous indignation when residents co-mingle their trash, his criticism masked by a smile as he sorts through tin cans and glass jars with meticulous attention.

The transfer station may not be pretty, but Bill knows its value. He opens each of Frank's bags and eyes its contents before tossing it into the dumpster. He stacks the cans in a shed at the edge of the transfer station, explaining that once he has accumulated enough, he will cash them in at the redemption center next to the grocery store. Frank has watched Bill dig through sofas discarded among the construction materials, collecting old coins. "Once I found a rosary at the bottom of a bag of discarded clothes," Bill brags. On his day off, he mans a booth at the local flea market, selling knick-knacks, paintings, and old furniture he rescues during the week.

Franks says: "I get it. You gotta be vigilant. I used to be in military security."

Bill dismisses the flatlander's comment. "Ain't got no use for the military. And the military ain't got no use for me."

At this impasse, the conversation changes to the catamount.

Bills says a friend spotted a catamount on his back property—or at least he saw suspicious tracks in the mud. "Whatcha think?" he asks Frank. Frank sighs. Dropping off a week's garbage can take an hour or two once Bill gets going.

The catamount, also known as the puma, mountain lion, panther, or cougar, was officially declared extinct in 2011, but rumors about the survival of the animal run rampant. West Brook has few claims to fame, but the catamount is paramount among them. A stuffed West Brook catamount, shot in 1875, is on permanent display at the Boston Museum of Science.

Frank angles to be the voice of reason. "I read that on Thanksgiving Day in 1881, a young boy noticed tracks in the snow. He shot the animal in the head. That, my friend, was the last catamount ever spotted in Vermont."

"If that was the last catamount in Vermont," Bill says, "I'm the last fucking Green Mountain boy." The tense muscles of his sinewy arms challenge this Yankee who dares to question the mountain lion sighting.

"You just might be right," Frank concedes, looking at his watch. Who cares that the last catamount killed in the state was shot in 1881? Accurate or not, catamounts bring out the fight in Vermonters. "Or maybe you're just high."

This tickles Bill's fancy. He raises a calloused hand for a high five. Frank rises to the challenge, a glimmer of victory in his skeptical eye.

Bill tells anyone who asks he's been sober for years, but an awful lot of his stories take place during his drinking days

"You know about the Green Mountain boys?" he asks. "A rugged crew, back-mountain, hard-drinking boys. They raised hell at the Catamount Tavern in Bennington in the 1700s. Right down the road from the Bennington monument."

"I've driven by," Frank says.

"The Green Mountains boys hung their hats there. Hung a few men there too."

Every native Vermonter knows the story, Bill says. The "Boys," led by Ethan Allen, formed an armed militia. When officials from New York tried to enforce their laws, the Green Mountain Boys took them on, sometimes administering a beating.

"The most rebellious race on the continent," Bills says with pride. "Put a stuffed catamount on the tavern's signpost to scare off the New Yorkers."

Frank turns off his ignition. This is going to take a while.

"Been thinking," Bill says, "a stuffed catamount might be just what we need around here."

Vermonters call West Brook lawless because the town is so small it does not require a sheriff. Bill sees things another way. "We make our own rules," he says, pulling a Snapple bottle from Frank's trash and setting it aside. He raises his eyebrows as if to say, "You see what I mean?"

"I don't take any guff." Bill is on a roll now. "Like the boys," he rests a boot on Frank's fender. "I'd take great pleasure in chasing away New Yorkers. And by New Yorkers, I mean all of you flatlanders," he says. "No offense intended." His throaty smoker's guffaw ends in a cough.

"You hear the one about the trooper?"

Bill and a friend were fishing on Lake Raponda when a Vermont State trooper arrived on the scene, looking for his canoe. He accused the two men of stealing his boat.

After some shouting, the two men came ashore and the officer on duty bounced his friend's face into the hood of his police cruiser. "He threatened to show us what police brutality was all about and said he was sick of white trash Vermonters and stupid potheads."

"I showed him a thing or two," Bill says. At the sentencing, a doctor said the trooper suffered from post-traumatic stress disorder. After Bill filed a civil suit, the trooper resigned from the State Police.

Best of all, Bill received $10,000 in the civil settlement.

"Still want to take me on?" Bill laughs.

Frank is speechless. He supposes the guy means no harm, but the discussion has taken a discomforting turn.

West Brook, like much of Vermont, functions under an uncomfortable truce between the hardy locals, who string together three jobs just to get by (like Bill), and intruders (like Frank) who hire locals to watch their—often empty—homes, mow their out-of-place lawns, and recycle their garbage.

"We should do some target shooting one of these days," Frank says.

In the day, Bill had been a carpenter, a damned good one. When Frank first purchased his vacation retreat, he hired Bill to reface the mildewed woodwork in his family room. Bill priced the job, demonstrating a craftsman's eye, and the two had batted around ideas for improvements. But in the months that followed, Bill never showed up to complete the job. Off on a drunken binge, Frank guessed. He assumed that target shooting was just as unlikely to happen. Still, Bill knew where he lived.

Frank tugs at his door. But even as he turns back on his ignition, he imagines Bill, belly up to the bar with those Green Mountain boys, a cold brewsky in his hand, launching into one of his many stories. Maybe the one about when he was twenty-two and working as a carpenter in Vernon. Bill didn't flinch when he described taking on those steelworkers. Not that he was a scab, mind you, but they insulted him. What choice did he have but to flatten their noses? In return, they beat the shit out of him, broke his left knee, and ripped the tendons in his right ankle.

He had to defend himself, understand? Bill tells this story with a chuckle, proud to stand his ground. The Green Mountain boys would understand. After all, they scared off the New Yorkers and chased the intruders from their land. Admittedly, some methods of coercion were questionable. When Dr. Samuel Adams, who owned land in the New Hampshire Grants, tried to defend the New Yorkers, the Green Mountain boys put him on trial at the Catamount Tavern and decided he was guilty. To punish him, they tied a chair to the tavern's sign and made him sit in the chair for hours.

Frank and Bill turn to look at the rusted dump sign. "Got plenty of old chairs in the back," Bill says.

"Fortunately," Frank says, "the Catamount Tavern burned down in 1871."

"The Green Mountain boys won the first battle of the American Revolution and founded the Republic of Vermont," Bill says. "Be careful who you mess with."

Frank puts his car into reverse.

"Good talking to you, Bill," he says, backing out with care. The April mud splashes in the rearview mirror as he retreats through the deep ruts.

Frank regrets not pointing out, all in good fun, of course, who pays Bill's salary.

Those damn New Yorkers, that's who.

The man was lucky that Frank's military discipline had taught him restraint.

But what was the point? Bill always got in the last word. In his stories, he wins every time. Engraved stones, brass plaques, Frank had seen them all, but were the framers of history and myth any more accurate in their portrayal of the forces that shaped this state, this nation, than the cantankerous keeper of the West Brook transfer station? Was the history they recorded any more to be trusted than Bill's tall tales?

Frank locks his car doors and turns onto the paved road, happy to be heading home. On the alert for catamounts lurking, he keeps his eyes on the side of the road where creatures wait silently for any invader who would dare to stuff them, place them in a museum, or swear to unreliable stories about their extirpation. As Frank drives through the dark woods, he is sure they watch his every move.

Back at the transfer station, Bill culls through detritus, salvaging what he can to cobble together a hard life in a cold climate. Chuckling, he awaits another second homeowner. Another unwelcome invader not to be trusted, who would listen to his stories, and leave their treasures behind.

# UNDER WATER

"She was one big motherfucker." The woman, rough-hewn and tough through and through, was standing at the counter of the country store to purchase her bear license. She had spotted her prey the previous evening. Pushing unkempt hair out of her eyes with a hand already scarred by prior battles, she towered over the cashier.

"What will you do with the bear if you shoot it?" The New Yorker next in line was skeptical. In Vermont to catch the last skiing of the season, he kept a safe distance from the woman whose ripe scent repelled him.

"Stew it, of course. I'd have enough meat for a year."

The towheaded boy who manned the counter made change with a lop-sided grin. He preferred the give and take of idle small-town gossip to high school, where the days went on too long and one had to sit still all day.

"Where did you see him?" the boy asked. He knew that hibernating animals were emerging for the season. Just yesterday, a red fox crossed his yard with a squirrel in its mouth, foraging for her young.

"Like I would tell you." No one was getting her bear.

The boy had the afternoon off. His best friend was waiting for him in the parking lot under the big American flag and next to the sign that said: "Parallel parkers will be shot." All angles and dark hair, his friend had spent much of the winter on a snowboard he made himself, surfaces shellacked to a frictionless sheen that carried him down the mountain so fast that the pine trees passed in a frenzied blur.

But now, spring had arrived. The two boys tussled like puppies as they walked the short two blocks to his house, kicking stones and jabbing at each other. As soon as they entered the yard, they pulled the kayak out of the musty shed where it languished next to the weed whacker, a half-empty gasoline can, and an unnecessary lawn mower. For much of the winter, well into spring, five feet of snow barricaded the door to the shed. Now they flung open the creaky wooden door and admitted the spring sun like a burst of enthusiasm.

The creek ran high with snowmelt. Deciduous trees budded; yellow-green leaves emerged by the moment. The day was practically hot, and the boys shed their unnecessary sweatshirts and dipped toes into the bracing water. The surface of the stream reflected more than enough suns to erase winter's memory.

"I've got the oars. Where are the life jackets?" the dark-haired boy asked, dragging the boat down the ramp.

His friend was already out the door. "Don't be a wuss. Let's get a move on." They had waited too long and were crazy to go.

A decisive push puts things in motion. One grunt as they gave the kayak a shove into the stream at the edge of the property; a celebratory shout as they leapt into the boat and dug oars into the roiling water. The current cast their lot downstream, leaving a winter's load of boredom behind. They attacked the white water with vigor, oars negotiating the clash between winter cold and spring heat, attempting to dictate terms for the seasonal struggle between what had been and what would be.

"Holy moly, guacamole." The dark-haired boy propelled the kayak from the back. The tow-haired boy directed the bow with an artful swipe of his oar.

Underneath overhanging branches that still lacked enough leaves to cast shadows, the kayak rolled from side to side. Currents eddied around rocks that later in the season would become sun-drenched islands for lolling swimmers but which now hid just below the surface with dark menace. They pushed the kayak first to one shore, then pulled it to the other, twirling madly between the two as the boys rode it like a roller coaster. They fought to maintain control.

"Whoa, nelly." Eyes wide open. Adrenaline pumping. No time for small talk. Even at this moment, in their prime, strong and sure of their power, the boys were only pawns in an epic battle between winter's melting snow and spring's surging vitality. A sinister swell rose to the side of the boat like a powerful bear protecting its young. The dark-haired boy defended with a flawless sweep stroke but came up short. With one decisive swat, the wave flipped the boat, rolling the vessel and dumping the boys with a splash into the foaming water.

"Grab the kayak!" The towheaded boy commanded, still thrilled as he the current carried him away. "Shit, it's freezing." The plastic hull was out of his friend's reach.

Their mouths formed little O's of wonder as the icy current pulled them downstream. Winter, which still lingered near the floor of the stream, held them in one last embrace.

On the shore, the woman held her gun at the ready. Her eyes trained on the bear on the other side of the stream where the hungry animal was scouting for passing fish, oblivious to danger as he followed his instinct for survival. When the kayak, with its clinging passenger, crashed into the rocks at his feet, the bear looked up in alarm. Did he see the gun? Did he glimpse the boy under the surface? Something spooked him.

"Goddamn," the woman cursed as the bear lumbered off into the woods. Only then did she look down and spot the blond boy under the water, blue eyes wide with terror. Setting down her rifle, she plowed into the current with a disgusted grunt, legs like tree trunks, hair like Medusa. She grabbed the boy's skinny arm, bruising it while yanking him to shore. Blue and trembling, the wet boy struggled to catch his breath.

"I had him," she said, "in my sight." She offered the boy her jacket, which carried within its matted fill a season's supply of sweat and smoke. "What the fuck were you doing out there without a life jacket?" She picked up her gun and looked off into the woods with regret.

The boy was terrified by the cold that gripped his chest. His lungs refused to expand. Burrowing into her woolen jacket, he was swallowed as if by a wild beast.

Stowing her gun in the backseat of a rusty, mud-stained car, the woman returned to the shivering boy, depositing him onto the candy-wrapper-strewn and duct-taped seat. She cranked the car's heater up high and poured coffee into the lid of her thermos. The cup she offered him was thick with sugar and cream. The woman who hunted alone would have been more comfortable with a bear carcass than this almost drowned boy who stunk up her car with creek water. Her next steps would have required less effort. Instead, warming at last, the boy asked: "Where is my friend?" The woman looked at him blankly. They were in this together now.

Downstream, the bear returned to the shore, still hungry. The woman and her passenger did not see the motionless animal as they drove the dirt road that ran parallel to the creek, eyes glued to the water with the intense focus of all expert hunters. They thought only of locating the dark-haired boy.

Two miles downstream, the second boy clung to an overhanging branch, sensation slowly ebbing from his limbs.

They stood silently on the side of the creek as EMTs placed the boy on a stretcher. The swirling lights of the ambulance competed with dappled sunshine that was already fading. Fiddlehead ferns, just about to unfurl, bowed their heads.

The towheaded boy watched from the shore. He turned down the EMT's offer of a blanket. He was already in good hands.

That summer, the blond-haired boy learned to hunt under the cranky tutorage of the wild-haired woman with the eagle eyes. Days, he still stood behind the counter of the store, but locals noticed he was less likely to chat, secretive almost in his silence as he made change. He smelled different, sweaty like a man after a day's labor. The customers kept their distance as they gathered up bags of overpriced groceries.

The dark-haired boy spent much of the summer on his front porch, a blanket over his knees on even the hottest of days. Nights, he tried to stay awake to avoid nightmares in which he always drowned. He had no interest in hunting, resisted unnecessary movement.

If, when the summer forest was thick with maturing leaves and ever darkening shadows, a shot rang out and an expertly aimed bullet downed the marauding bear, the huntress and her protégé were not about to tell. For them too, it was a matter of survival.

# CONSTANCE

A white flash. A thunderous boom. "What the hell?" Despite Ken's increasing deafness, the loud bang pulled him from his deepest sleep, disrupting those first three hours of total surrender before anxiety, restlessness and the perpetual need to pee roused him. He spoke without totally waking. Audrey echoed, "What was that?" but he didn't hear, nor would he remember talking with her in the morning.

The crash could have been fireworks, a gunshot, an electrical short.

He resumed snoring lightly, rhythmically.

The elderly couple had climbed into bed at nine p.m. with the loft window wide open. Ken made a stab at reading his novel. "I'm on page 45. What page are you on?" he asked, a bedtime ritual. By the time Audrey replied "75," her eyes were already beginning to close. She kissed the air, her long gray braid stretched out beside her.

After the blast, Audrey lay in the dark room, listening for an explanation. She sniffed for smoke, any sign of danger. She listened for voices, aahs of appreciation, cries of fear, and then rolled over and examined the clock. It read five minutes before 11:00. For half an hour, she waited for the approach of emergency vehicles, but the night was quiet, clueless. She tiptoed to the window but could only make out a few raindrops snaking down the windowpane and darkness.

When they rose the next morning, there was no sign of a disturbance. A few cars sped by, carrying their occupants to work at the local ski resort. She drank coffee on the living room couch and watched the *Today* show. Ken rode his exercycle in the basement, watching season two of *Deadwood*. Despite the subtitles, he cranked the volume up high. Bawdy saloon chatter competed with snippets of news. Matt Lauer regurgitated the latest human-interest story pervading the internet. The cats prowled the baseboards, sniffing for mice.

"You'd really like this show," Ken said, coming upstairs to take a bathroom break.

"I doubt it."

"The western setup is just a veneer. The show is really about morality and the attempt to civilize a chaotic mining town."

"All I hear is cursing. Motherfucker this. Motherfucker that."

"That's the thing. The show gives that word multiple meanings. It's all strange. In the center of town, the Chinese have a pig pen. That's where the murdered bodies disappear."

He always tried to convince her she was missing out. She didn't share his interest in watching hours of TV shows and often wondered if actors were more real to him than friends or family. She preferred a good book, or had before her eyes began to fail. Despite her thick glasses, she struggled now to get her right eye to coordinate with the left. If she read for too long without taking a break, her head throbbed in protest.

"Did you hear that explosion last night?" she asked him. "Maybe a transformer blew. I half expected the electricity to go out."

"Late last night?"

"I don't know. It was late for fireworks."

It had seemed like the middle of the night to them, but she realized that 11:00 p.m. was not that late for kids on a summer night.

"Strange." His favorite adjective. A lot of things seemed strange to him these days. He headed back downstairs to South Dakota. Last week he'd spent hours watching *The Wire*. He compared everything to *Dexter*.

After his show ended, they headed out to take their dog, Henry, for their regular morning walk. Ken was still describing going-ons in the bar. She was looking for signs of what had occurred during the night.

They had retired to a second home community in Vermont several years before. At any point in time, two-thirds of the houses on their block were empty. Occupancy patterns were seasonal, skiers in the winter, vacationing teachers in the summer. The larger the house, the less often the lights were on.

Trailing Henry's meandering path along the dirt road, she looked for detritus. Ken rattled off plot developments. She saw no signs of fire, no firecrackers or duds. All was quiet at the blue house on the corner, which looked out over a fire pond to an impressive span of the Green Mountains.

No need to leash the dog. These roads were seldom traveled.

He described the viewer campaign to revive *Deadwood*. There was no cable in rural Vermont, only satellite and mail-order Netflix.

She nodded, uninterested.

They completed their accustomed circuit, up Pine Hill, left on Sawmill Road, down the main (and only paved) road of the development. Unannounced, out of nowhere, a large dusty white bus careened down the road, miles over the speed limit. The type of "luxury coach" used by tourists to view seasonal attractions. The mammoth vehicle barely missed the ambling dog; massive tires launched stones into their path like shrapnel flying from a bomb. Pine branches trembled in its wake.

"What the hell?" Ken asked (again).

The bus turned left onto their block, raising a cloud of dirt and dust. To their amazement, it pulled over in front of a wooded lot that adjoined their property. After a brief pause, the passenger door wheezed open. In a silent column, passengers, each as pale as Vermont in February, headed into the woods.

"How strange," he commented. The tourists exiting the bus wore costumes from an earlier time. The men wore wrinkled, mud-stained hunting gear, well-worn earth-toned shirts buttoned up to tight collars. Baggy pants with ankle-high boots and wide-brimmed hats. Belts with slots for bullets. Many of the men had mustaches that appeared to be authentic.

The women wore summer dresses, lace dipping below their knees. Long hair tied severely like Amish or Mormon wives enjoying a respite from the hard work of farming or providing food for the family table.

A large, sturdy-looking woman led the crowd, a half-smile of anticipation on her handsome face. The woman chatting at her side looked familiar to Audrey, despite her old-timey dress. The other costumed visitors followed the two women, their steps lively without the usual confusion of crowds. They knew where they were going.

Ken and Audrey watched in fascination, the spectacle as engrossing as TV, as nuanced as a good book.

The passengers waded into the waist-high greenery, quickly taken in by ferns and Queen Anne lace, snagged by the burdocks' explosive spines as they disappeared from the side of the road into a bank of blackberry bushes. Only the tops of the tallest men's heads were still visible from the side of the road.

The bus driver got out of the coach, lighting his cigarette before his feet hit the ground. "Hey folks," he greeted the elderly couple.

"You almost killed us back there!" Ken remonstrated, his teacher's voice reconstituted after all these years.

The driver chuckled. Smoke billowed from his mouth with each exhalation. "Sorry about that. Not used to country roads."

Henry headed into the bushes, hot on the tourists' trail.

"What's going on?" Having received his apology, Ken's curiosity took over.

"Family reunion," the bus driver informed them. "The old family homestead is somewhere out there," gesturing to the field, "or used to be as I understand it." He left the bus running. As the dust settled, exhaust and cigarette smoke took its place.

"Oh, I know where that is!" Audrey piped up. "I see the remnants of the cellar hole from our bathroom window."

"Aah." The driver was clearly unimpressed.

"That must be the Potter family! And that was Constance from the Historical Society in the lead, dressed up like in the olden days." She turned to her husband. "You know, Constance from the library! She's related to the Potter family on her father's side. She once told me that her mother, a nurse from New York, could never adjust to life in the boonies. The Potters have been here for hundreds of years. There's a road named after them behind the dump."

She closed her eyes to remember what Constance had told her. "This whole mountainside used to be their farm, over a hundred acres. An apple orchard, a few dozen sheep." During the census, Constance had walked around the block with her, inquiring which homes were occupied by full-timers. Audrey had shared what little she knew about the second homeowners, and in exchange, Constance had related tidbits of local history. "The forest used to be clear cut from here down to Route 100. The Potter house sat on top of the hill overlooking the slope."

Local history was Constance's passion. "Maple Grove had a militia company in the early years which used to drill in June on the cleared fields of the Potter farm," she told them

"Unfortunately," Constance concluded, "early in the 20th century, lightning struck the barn. The house caught fire and burned to the ground. After the fire, a large lumber company purchased the property for their mill." Later, in response to the rapid growth of the ski industry, a developer parsed the hillside into the one-acre lots. The "planned community," where Audrey and Ken now lived.

*Seeds for a mini-series*, Ken said, but without the drama. "What are they doing down there?" He asked the driver, looking out into the field.

"Don't have a clue," the bus driver threw his cigarette to the ground, grinding it into the dirt. "Just hope they don't stay out there too long. I'm supposed to be back at the lodge for lunch by 12:30. Every highway in this damn state is under construction. I can't go five miles without being held up by flagmen. It drives me crazy."

The dog emerged from the bushes, briars in his coat, tail wagging madly. Down the hill, they heard the distant voices of the bus's passengers, the low laughter of women and men's voices in conversation. When the volume rose, they surmised the family was heading back towards the bus. Audrey considered waiting to greet her friend but did not want to intrude.

"Take it easy," Ken said to the bus driver.

"I would love to know what the story is," Audrey confided to Ken as they headed back to the house.

"Would have been more dramatic if they had arrived in model T's, *like i*n the 20s." Nucky Thompson in Boardwalk Empire in his smart suit. "Or maybe in a stagecoach." That tour bus was anachronistic. "In any case, I prefer to watch dramas from a more comfortable vantage point. In one hour episodes and preferably accompanied by a glass of wine," he told her, amusing only himself.

As soon as they were home, Audrey sat down at her PC to google the Potters. Unfortunately, Ken decided at the same time to review their Netflix queue. Last night, they watched *The Affair* together. It was difficult to select a show which appealed to them both. With only spotty DSL and limited bandwidth, Audrey watched the swirling icon going around and around.

"I'm off to the library," she announced in frustration. Driving down Cherry Hill Road, she heard the omnipresent sound of buzz saws. Late summer, skiers were busy putting away firewood for the winter. Some houses already had large piles of wood ready for stacking. Each year, more lots were cleared for construction. Newcomers seeded suburban lawns destined to be buried in three feet of snow for half the year.

At the Maple Grove library, the librarian told Audrey that Constance had called in sick. In the library's collection of local history, Audrey uncovered a file folder of restored photographs. Edith Potter—although the picture was taken in 1915, the resemblance to Constance was striking—stood triumphantly, holding a rifle next to a bear hanging on the porch of the local hotel. In the second, the Potter brothers (in knit caps and holding rifles) showed off their "trophies," two stags hanging from a branch propped horizontally between adjacent trees. Before filing away the photos, another image, taken in 1940, caught her attention. In the "Arms Store float," a 1940 Chevy truck with a pig on the roof headed down Main Street as part of the 4th of July day parade.

Audrey looked out the window of the library at the skate park. The library book group had read a gruesome book about two Vermont adolescents who had murdered a Hanover couple in cold blood for the sport of it. As Audrey watched now, two pimpled boys took turns riding up the ramp and flying out over the concrete pad.

The librarian waved as she left the library. "Did you find what you were looking for?"

"Absolutely," Audrey chirped. As a flatlander, Audrey often felt like an outsider. Unlike Ken, who missed the city, she had no desire to be anywhere else. But today there was something just below the surface, a hint of danger (the unexplained sound in the night, the photos of the Potters brandishing rifles, the buzz of saws that followed her down the road). What was the point of the pig on the roof?

Ken was in a tizzy when she got home. "It's about time." He looked meaningfully at the clock. He liked supper at five.

"That guy up the block has been mowing his lawn all afternoon. It's driving me crazy. Henry has been barking non-stop." As Ken complained, they heard a loud thud, felt the quake of a towering pine falling to the ground, followed by the renewed grinding of a buzz saw. "I can't hear the TV over the incessant noise."

Audrey took husks off the corn she was preparing for dinner, gazing out the kitchen window. The birch, pines, and hemlock, she thought, had long ago swallowed up the Potters' farm, erasing a family's history. The house she occupied was the latest chapter in a complicated book. Looking out at the compost bin next to their shed, scarred by the claws of the local bear, she imagined Mrs. Potter in her lacy finery, rifle in hand, the bear hanging at her side.

That night, she had difficulty going to sleep. For several hours, she waited for another explosion, but heard nothing except the owl's call. "Who cooks for you?"

She wandered the darkened house. Outside, a full moon illuminated the pines. At 2 a.m., she looked out the window towards the adjacent property. What she saw caused her to grab the windowsill to steady herself. The spotlight of the August super moon illuminated the site of the abandoned cellar hole. The stones that staked the Potter's claim glowed in the moon's brilliance. In the middle of the former homestead, a small army of men and women stood upright like meerkats. Rifles held aloft, like pioneers protecting their land. From whom? The wildlife that had once inhabited it? The current residents who vacationed where the settlers had once farmed?

Or was it just a dream, she asked herself later, turning over in her bed in the loft, listening to Ken's snoring and envying his deafness. Her book was still open on the bed beside her. What page was she on? She wondered. Had Ken even remembered to ask before passing out at her side? Her eyes ached from trying to focus. She closed the lids gratefully and felt the pressure ease. Unable to make any sense of what she thought she had seen, she fell asleep.

*****

"Henry's taken off."

When Audrey came down the stairs the next morning, Ken had made coffee. "I let him out to do his business, and he just took off."

The dog, set in his ways, was not a wanderer. A daily walk satisfied him. Otherwise, he was content to lie at their feet chewing on a bone. Audrey gulped her coffee as she pulled on jeans. She had an idea where the dog might have gone.

Ken said: "He'll come back when he's hungry."

"Says the man who worries about ticks and bears in the woods."

Strapping on hiking shoes, Audrey walked up the road, calling out Henry's name. When she arrived at the spot where the sight-seeing bus had parked the previous day, she easily located the trampled weeds where the Potters had descended into the bushes. Continuing to call for the dog, she followed their tracks through the blackberry bushes towards the cellar hole. As was her habit, she stamped her feet. A PBS special about bears had suggested that hikers in the woods announce their presence.

Before she approached the ruins, the undergrowth thinned. She smelled char and saw a tall maple at the corner of the lot with a black cavity scarring its western side. At last, Audrey had discovered the source of the mysterious boom two nights before. For the second time, lightning had struck the Potter's land.

Only a few steps away, half-buried stones marked the footprint of the cellar, unobtrusive in the morning light. Henry, digging in a far corner of the foundation, greeted her with a wildly wagging tail but with no intention of abandoning his fervent undertaking. Audrey looked west over what had once been farmland. Where there had once been a cleared field, there was now a confusion of leaves, tree trunks, a tangle of vines. Sunlight filtered through branches like an intruder, shedding little illumination. The slope was steep, of no use to anybody now. The Potters must have worked hard to claim it.

"Henry, stop that." The dog didn't look up as Audrey approached. He had piled soil and stones behind him, clawing at a hole about a foot deep. Pulling him by his collar, Audrey examined his work, suspecting that this excavation had existed prior to their arrival. Henry was not a dog that buried things. Something had attracted him to this spot.

Had the Potters, during their visit, discovered something from the past? Or had they buried something of their own? A remembrance, a time capsule to document their time in this place? Why now, long after the property had been sold and reclaimed, not only by nature but by second home-owning flatlanders who wanted nothing more than a little peace? The coincidence of the recent lightning strike, followed by the descendant's unlikely visit and her late-night vision of the pioneers defending their land, unsettled her.

Dragging Henry back up the now well-trodden path, Audrey barely noticed the ripe berries ready for picking.

By the time she arrived home with the dog, Ken was on his exercycle again. He had just started the final season of his series. From the basement, she could hear the bar owner saying, "Don't I yearn for the days a draw across the throat made for a fuckin' resolution." Civilization, Ken informed her, was creeping into the camp. Before finishing her breakfast, Audrey took a long shower. Who knew what she may have picked up in the woods? Poison ivy was insidious this time of year.

*****

That night, the couple compromised on the evening's activity, playing a game of scrabble. Ken, a master at using up all his tiles, hooted with pride when he formed the word "televise." Before falling to sleep, Audrey pulled up her white sheet, wrapping herself as if in a shroud. She read the book she had picked up at the library: Maple Grove, Vermont, Exposing the past as she drifted off to sleep. She dreamed about land grants, hunting rifles, and animals displayed as trophies. Her husband slept restlessly, wrestling with loose ends. Without glasses, she could not see his tears. In his deafness, he was oblivious to her sighs. He did not hear the footsteps in the woods behind their house. She did not see Constance camped out in the cellar hole, rifle at the ready, prepared to protect family property from the dishonorable claims of uninvited intruders.

# VEGANS ON THE APPALACHIAN TRAIL

Stella dipped her bloody toes into the clear, cool water of the pond. Her toenails were blue. Where blisters had broken open, raw sores wept. In the distance, a loon cried. Behind her, day hikers roosted on rocks. The white-haired woman ignored them and waited for the water to numb her aching feet. She rooted in her backpack for something to eat.

August was almost over. If she had stayed on schedule, she would have summited Mt. Washington by now. Instead, she was barely into Vermont. This morning, she had crossed over Stratton Mountain where the ski resort's gondola carried summer vacationers to the fire tower with its panoramic views of three states. Stella hadn't bothered to climb the tower's rickety stairs. She paused at the mountain's summit, looking for blazes that showed the northern route down.

The mountain's caretaker emerged from his small cabin, extending his hand. He greeted her and asked where she was heading.

"Heading?" She resented the intrusion, her own hands embedded in her pockets.

"On your journey. Which way are you going?"

"My journey?"

"Are you heading north or south?" The caretaker was used to the disorientation of through hikers. After many years on the mountain, he had learned to speak slowly, especially to hikers who, like the elderly Stella, were struggling. Most of this year's through hikers had summited his mountain in July, stragglers earlier in August.

"North. I am heading north," Stella snapped.

With a sigh, he pointed out the trailhead. Stella plowed her way past the gawking tourists. From the trail, she could see the gondola landing. A wedding party was assembling to watch the bride and groom say their vows on the mountain top.

Two hours later, the sun now high in the sky, she descended to the small sandy beach at Stratton Pond. To make her day's goal, Manchester Village, she had many more hours of walking in front of her. Her lunch break would have to be brief.

As she dangled her throbbing feet into the coolness of the pond's water, two hikers approached from the north and plopped down beside her. Unlike Stella, singular and silent, they were hiking together and chatted as they searched their backpacks for provisions.

"I am so hungry," the first declared, a stocky young woman with her hair cut short. Her sleeveless t-shirt revealed arms festooned with tattoos. She wore thick socks and serious hiking boots. She set out a feast of bread and cheese, fresh fruit and chocolate bars.

"Appalachian Trail?" the second hiker asked Stella.

"Yep," Stella answered. She spoke only to through hikers, expecting the most dedicated to understand. At least these two didn't look at her like she was a lost cause.

"I'm Trudy," the young woman extended her hand. "We're hiking south on the Long Trail. This is my friend, Les."

Stella finished her lunch: almonds and dried fruit.

"Vegan?" Les asked. Slender and athletic, the second hiker was of indeterminate sexuality, a soft-spoken gay man or perhaps transitioning.

"Yep."

"Me too," Trudy said. "But for the sake of this hike, I've taken a holiday. There is just no way I can get enough calories without eating meat. They serve the most awesome bacon at the Manchester hut."

Trudy and Les were easily fifty years younger than Stella. "I have eaten nothing with a face for twenty years," the older woman told them.

"Far out. Respect."

Young people, even those with the best of intentions, lacked any commitment to their convictions, Stella thought, but at least these two seemed sincere.

"What brought you to the trail?" Les asked, a frequent hiker's inquiry.

"I'm hiking for elephants," Stella explained. An activist from D.C., she was raising money for a worthy cause. Friends and former students had pledged their support. Her trek was not just a personal challenge, but a means to an end. "I started a GoFundMe page in October. So far, I have raised almost $5000." As she spoke, her voice became stronger. "As a professor at Washington U, I visited Africa many times. The plight of the elephants is desperate."

"I have fresh moleskin if you need some," Les said, pointing to Stella's battered feet rippling beneath the water.

"No need," Stella replied, buoyed by lunch and the opportunity to state her goal. "I better get going." Pulling her feet from the pond water, she searched through her backpack. Despite the padding of thick socks tailored for hiking, putting her boots back on was no mean feat. Trudy and Les watched as she angled her dying toenails into the battered boots.

Trudy inhaled as if preparing to speak, but Stella's fierce glare repelled any offer of help. Instead, Trudy said, "We're heading South on the Long Trail. Over Stratton mountain and to the state line. We're almost there. Back to school next month."

Stella preferred silence to Trudy's meat-fueled exuberance. She picked up the sturdy branch she had adopted as a hiking stick months ago in the Blue Ridge Mountains at the beginning of her journey. Now she used it to balance as she shifted her weight onto aching feet. Unable to stifle a guttural groan, she collapsed back down onto the rocky shore with a defeated thud. Pain shot up her spindly legs. Months of walking had carved them down to skin and bone. Stars swam in front of her eyes. A wave of nausea overcame her.

Trudy and Les scurried to her side. "Are you okay?"

Stella caught her breath. A hawk tattooed on Trudy's tanned hand seemed to fly in front of her face. Confused, the water of the pond appeared to fill the deep blue sky. Les's arm enveloped her, at once her daughter's goodbye embrace and the constraint of the seat belt that had not saved her husband when his Ferrari slammed into a brick wall.

"Shit," she said. She had hundreds of miles to go.

Her feet throbbed. She could feel the warmth of blood or pus seeping into her socks.

"For the elephants…" she said, "I have to go on."

Trudy checked her phone for a connection. There was none.

"What you've got to do is take a load off," Les said. With gentle hands, the quiet hiker once again removed Stella's boots. Stella, reduced to helplessness, examined the hiker's flat chest, the baby-like down on the young person's chin.

"What are you?" she asked. Les squeezed a worm of triple antibiotic lotion onto the top of Stella's right big toe and then massaged it into the inflamed skin of her feet.

"A friend," Les said.

"No, I mean girl, boy, what?"

Still massaging, Les answered, "Inside or out?"

Stella felt her frustration growing even as the pain in her feet subsided. "I need to get to Manchester tonight," she said. She had planned her hike meticulously. Although she had fallen behind, she never wandered from the route she had plotted.

"She's a girl," Trudy snapped, "just not born that way. We've got to get you some help."

Stella mulled this over. She would take it slower this time. If she could just stand, she could be on her way. "I'll take you up on that moleskin," she said.

Trudy said, "There's a caretaker on the summit of the mountain. I'm sure he has medical supplies."

"He's south. I'm heading north," Trudy insisted.

"You can hardly walk. Let us give you a hand. We'll help you back up the mountain. The caretaker can call for a medic. Then you'll be on your way."

It did not surprise Stella that a vegan who ate meat could so easily propose a pivot. The former professor of anthropology had no patience for people who said one thing and did another.

"Trudy's right," Les said, holding her feet as she would a wounded pet. "You need to take care of yourself."

Stella's sweatshirt hung on her emaciated body. She had lost weight during the hike. Not only had the trek battered her feet, but bruises covered her legs; her back ached. The trip up the mountain would only take an hour or two. The girl's help, as much as she hated to admit it, would make the ascent possible.

"There's a phone tower up there," Trudy added. "While you are resting up, you can call your family."

She let the comment go by, unacknowledged. She had accepted medical assistance, nothing more.

The pain of the hike up the mountain was unrelenting. Her frustration at retracing steps for no reason was unforgiving. Trudy supported Stella from the left side, bearing as much of her weight as she was able. Les guided her from the right, her hand cupping the elderly woman's elbow. They ambled without speaking. As they approached the summit of Stratton Mountain, the gondola from the ski resort once again came into view. The wedding party had dispersed from the scenic overlook, their vows complete. The guests now stood in a cacophonous crowd waiting for the gondola to take them back down the mountain to the reception in the resort below. Stella concentrated on breathing. Like a woman giving birth, she tried to counter the agony of every step with the distraction of rhythmic inhales and exhales.

They arrived at the fire tower by late afternoon.

"You're back," the mountain's caretaker said to her. This time, his hands hung at his side.

"She needs help," Trudy said, checking her phone for messages.

Stella glared at the young woman but could not stand up on her own. Instead, she allowed the two girls to walk her to the caretaker's hut. He pulled out a wooden chair and positioned it in front of the wood stove.

"Thanks." The caretaker introduced himself as Artie and put water on for tea. His hut was no larger than her office at the university. It contained a cot, a cluttered wooden desk, the chair, and a hot plate. A burly man in his sixties, Artie seemed unconcerned.

"We can get a doctor up here, if you like, or medivac you down to the clinic."

"I don't think that's necessary. I need to get back to hiking as soon as I can."

"Yes, I know. Your journey. Up here, we all have one."

Artie gave her a mug of hot tea and a plate of shortbread cookies. Stella's stomach grumbled as she fought the desire to eat one buttery cookie after another. She was ravenous. The caretaker had no way of knowing she was a vegan. He would not judge her if she ate a few. The girls had left her in his care while they climbed up the fire tower to check out the view. The visibility from the tower, Artie told her, was almost endless. No one would ever know if Stella violated her own restrictions, just this once. Trudy and Les were, after all, responsible for her heading in the wrong direction.

As part of Artie's job responsibilities, he told her, twice a day he climbed the tower to look for fires in the Green Mountains. "Don't know why," he said. "One time I spotted a plume of smoke rising from the forest and called a local farmer to notify him. I waited for him to call back and tell me he had it under control. When I didn't hear from him, I called again. He said, 'You were right. There's a fire, sure enough.' Not long after, the fire burned itself out. Things have a way of taking care of themselves."

When Artie was not spotting fires, he helped hikers like her find their way. Several trails crossed the mountain's summit. He pointed them in the right direction.

The hot tea, the buttery cookies, the memory of the girls' support, and Artie's calm reflections, the whole set-up lulled Stella into complacency. When almost inhuman fortitude was required of her, her eyelids became heavy as the man talked about journeys and the many hikers he had helped.

She dreamed she joined the wedding reception, and all the celebrants cheered the successful completion of her journey. Les wore a stunning designer wedding gown, and Trudy played bass in the rock and roll band. Artie held out his hand and asked Stella to dance. She did, so light on her feet she could almost fly.

Elephants looked in from an enclosure outside. Their enormous eyes, heavily lashed, seemed wise and full of regret. They waited for her to come to their rescue.

When she woke up, a doctor stood in the hut's door. A smug vacationer staying at the resort, dressed in Bermuda shorts and a Yankees cap, who arrived via the gondola. He looked at her feet and clucked his tongue, took her temperature, looked at his watch. The distance she had traveled already was admirable, he said, but it was time to stop. He insisted she abandon the hike.

Les listened to the doctor's prognosis, stroking her smooth chin as if deep in thought. Trudy asked about the fate of the elephants. Besides being a sometimes vegan, Trudy was an animal right's activist. The tattoo on her right hand, she explained, was a tribute to the injured hawks at the sanctuary where she volunteered. She wanted to know what she could do to help.

Stella had no choice but to call her daughter. After going into detail about the elaborate arrangements the trip would require (babysitters, rescheduled meetings, a deferred appointment with the pediatrician), Cynthia agreed to fly up to Vermont the next morning to take her mother home.

Stella spent the night with Artie. After they had watched the heavens for a while, he handed her a map from his desk drawer. The offering meant nothing to him, but to her, it meant everything. He showed her the route north, explaining that many fingers had walked across the map. It barely held together now, but the caretaker assured her it had matured and softened with time.

"Next year, maybe you can go on a safari," her daughter said the next morning as she led her hobbling mother to the gondola, now empty of tourists and day trippers. Stella could not tell if her daughter was being facetious, but she assured her she already had plans.

Later, they sat on a plane which idled at the airport gate. Stella googled high-calorie vegan hiking food on her phone, discovering several excellent websites. "After Les recovers from reassignment surgery, we'll plan next summer's journey. Trudy says we can easily complete the last leg of the AT if we start at the Massachusetts border in June."

Cynthia nodded without taking her eyes off the tiny monitor in the seat in front of her where, via satellite, passengers could study the plane's trajectory. A broken red line designated the route to their intended destination. The simplified line flashed, of no interest to her mother at her side.

Still wearing hiking shoes over bandaged feet, Stella was already heading in the opposite direction. She would not let the elephants down. Next year, she and her friends would make it to the summit of Mt. Katahdin or bust.

# MISE EN PLACE

Joe stood in our front yard in his underpants, watering the peonies. I was leaving for work. Maybe I should have said something—for example: put your clothes on—but I was running late. Joe was a grown man, and I had no intention of taking over for his mother, a tight-mouthed farmer's wife who treated me like one in a long string of disappointments.

Joe had been on disability for ten years. While working for Northeast Utilities, he had been electrocuted while installing a junction box twenty feet up a pole. He had never fully recovered. His back chronically ached and his arms were numb. His list of complaints went on and on. When his doctor refused to write him any more prescriptions, he found his own ways of dealing with the pain. He spent one whole summer drinking with our next-door neighbor Ralph, riding shotgun in his pickup truck. When it came time for Ralph to go back into rehab, Joe latched on to a dozen new friends who had the schedule of his disability checks down pat. That time, I moved back in with my mom, but it was a disaster. I came back when Joe promised he had things under control.

My boss, Emile, insisted that restaurant employees report to work at noon to prepare the mise en place. Emile had ambitions. Most restaurants in Vermont were lucky if they filled half a dozen tables midweek, but Emile believed Yelp would put us on the map. We waitresses had our hands full. Customers expected us to smile in amusement while their kids dumped out sugar packets one by one as their parents grilled us on the provenance of the evening's vegetables. (Hint: in January in Vermont, the kitchen garden is two feet under snow.) Emile remained convinced that if he prepared cuisine with love, customers would reward us. Emile liked to chat with the "locals". He affected a country drawl when he talked with the kitchen staff and collected local sayings. "If you don't like the weather, just wait fifteen minutes," he said when we clustered at the window, worrying about driving home on the icy roads. "Got to, no one else will," he said with a grin when a customer told him to "take care." He was cute and sincere, and we forgave him for his condescension and, in return, he let us keep our tips.

That night Emile used the ingredients in the root cellar to make a "local" winter stew. Wardsboro's elementary school kids had recently completed a lobbying campaign in Montpelier to name the Gilfeather Turnip the State Vegetable. The entire sixth-grade class, all eight of them, had gone to the capital to see the proclamation signed by the Governor. The Town Council erected signs naming our little town the "Home of the Gilfeather Turnip."

"So, ladies," Emile said as we stood the counter peeling, "where do you suggest I start?"

I'd never cooked a turnip in my life. Couldn't stand them. Give me a bowl of cereal and an armchair in front of the TV and I'm content.

"Butter?" Sheila suggested. Smart girl, she knew every dish that Emile cooked started with butter and ended with a reduction laced onto the plate like filigree surrounding a precious gemstone.

"The Friends of the Library sell a book of turnip recipes," I contributed. "Everything from soup to desserts." I scored points once by bringing in *The Official Vermont Maple Cookbook*. Emile prepared a variation of every recipe in the book, two of which earned him four stars on Yelp.

In the end, Emile concocted a turnip soup, rich in butter and cheese, and served it with garlic bread. Only five of the ten tables in the dining room were filled that night, but the customers appeared happy. They usually were when Emile served comfort food disguised as nouvelle cuisine. Every time we delivered a plate hot from the kitchen, he asked us to emphasize the local origins of the dish.

"Mud season is a local specialty too," Sheila hissed as she held the kitchen door for me.

I smiled, balancing two plates and hoping that the overflowing stew wouldn't burn my forearm. Emile gave us the leftovers at the end of the evening. "A treat for la famille," he said, forgetting his drawl and falling back on his cooking school French.

I imagined he thought I had a bushel of rosy-cheeked kids still at home, not a boyfriend turning gray from long-term opiate abuse.

Joe and I met at the post office when I worked behind the counter. My kids were still in high school. At first, I thought he was just another Connecticut second-home owner, with his booming hellos and PO Box filled with legal correspondence. With time, he told me about his accident, the months in the hospital, his inability to keep up with the mortgage. He'd stand at the counter, watching me with those puppy dog eyes, like any mutt angling for a home.

My kids had moved out of state, as kids raised in Vermont so often do. I was lonely. My chats with Joe over the postal counter evolved into dinners in my kitchen. Despite his chronic pain and sporadic bouts of confusion, Joe was an appreciative guest. When he pointed out the waste of paying two rents, I didn't disagree.

We had a few good years. We visited my kids in their city apartments. Their dad, my high school sweetheart, had moved to California when they were small, following a nubile, blonde skier he met at Mount Snow while working on the grounds crew. Raised on absence, my children warmed to Joe's booming laughter and his bear-like hugs.

"That Sara," he said after visiting my daughter, "she's a pistol like her mom." I assumed he meant my daughter got her spirit from me, but I preferred to think she had my toughness, my determination to survive.

I wanted to be all that for him. Home, security, and simple, non-addictive pleasures.

My adult son, Felipe, was wary. "He's drinking a lot," he said, studying my face for a reaction.

"You would too if your body was wracked with pain," I answered. As a young boy, Felipe had massaged my feet. Now he had his own children to care for, and I wasn't about to look to him for sympathy. "He's got it under control," I said, tickling my granddaughter's fat pink foot until she dissolved into a giggly puddle of joy.

Junkies believe their lies. So must the people who try to love them.

When I needed a break, I filled the car with gifts for the grandkids and visited Sara or Felipe. Two years ago, I spent most of the summer babysitting

Sara's cats while she attended cooking school. Sara introduced me to Emile and his partner, Robert. They were considering opening a restaurant "up north." We'd drink wine in Sara's minuscule apartment and discuss Vermont. Given my homesickness, I played up its charms. I blame Narcan. If Joe hadn't thought he could push things, he might have stayed on track. When I agreed to move back in, he'd promised to cut off the opportunistic friends who were the source of his oxycodone. He made a point of telling me he'd had enough of constipation, nausea, the nights when he woke up in a terrified sweat.

"Doc's put me on a regimen of low-dose morphine," he said. "I don't need to be high. Just enough to take the edge off."

I returned to Vermont. Joe was penitent. He bought me a car, a used convertible, and we drove to the Dummerston Apple Festival. Two thousand pies and five hundred bikers. Joe put his arm around me. Despite his physical deterioration, he was almost a foot taller than me. "Darling, I am so glad you're home," he said. The leaves burned orange like in every movie you have ever seen set in New England in the fall.

"Me too."

Emile and Robert moved to Vermont and opened their restaurant. The US Post office, in a perpetual financial crisis, was merging their rural routes, and no longer had a job for me. Emile agreed to hire me. Joe and I celebrated my new job with a bottle of champagne and a sunset viewed from the half-filled hot tub on our back deck. Joe didn't slur his words, not once.

"Home," I decided. "This is home." By the end of the evening, Joe was visibly blurry around the edges, but he didn't pass out until he had held me in his arms for a blissful hour. In Vermont, warmth is a desirable asset.

Joe kept a cache of pills in his bedroom drawer, which he pressed between two spoons and snorted with a sneaky grin. I poured myself a glass of wine. "To each their own," he said. No matter how hard I worked, his disability check was more than my paycheck. Without him, I could not pay the rent on our cozy two-bedroom house.

All winter, Emile insisted the restaurant could succeed, despite a balance sheet that predicted doom. His partner, Robert, sat at one of the empty tables in the back, going over the books with a strained smile on his face. He bemoaned the lack of winter farmers' markets. Just in time, the first signs appeared on utility poles announcing the imminent re-opening of the spring markets. Emile was ecstatic. He danced a jig around the kitchen. I watched him rejoice, knowing he would find an ample supply of maple syrup at those markets, maybe a few greenhouse tomatoes at exorbitant cost, but never enough for a meal.

Joe hardly ever left the house. When I arrived home, the lights were always lit. He said he couldn't live without the pills. I couldn't live without him. I watched the melting snow for signs of spring. By May, green shoots appeared in the mud in front of my porch.

My peonies were my pride and joy. Peonies need a sunny location. Towering pines and groves of hemlock surrounded our house. We waged a never-ending battle against the encroachment of seedlings and monstrous ferns. That spring, Joe made a point of trimming back the branches overhead, guaranteeing sun in my garden. When the peony stalks reached three feet tall, he staked each one individually.

An addict, I told myself, would not show so much care, could not sustain such vigilance. He wouldn't be able to contribute to the rent or buy me a car.

Joe first shot heroin in June when the sun lingered on the horizon late into the evening. "It's like Oxy," he told me, "Only cheaper." He knew how to use a syringe because his father had needed to medicate animals on the farm. "I'm no fool," he assured me, "but those animals didn't have to suffer. Why should I?"

Mud season dried up the restaurant's business. We were lucky when three of the tables were filled. In the kitchen, Emile glowered at the stove, frantic for fresh greens, and checking his Yelp ratings four times a day. Sheila quit, accepting a job at the local diner. It was just the three of us now, Emile, Robert and me. The streams were overflowing. Emile said he missed New York, the energy, that endless line of customers.

"New York has its problems too," I reminded him. My grandchildren sent me crayon drawings with "I love you gramma" scrawled in red, drunken letters. Felipe asked when I was going to visit the city. I was ashamed to admit I couldn't leave Joe alone.

The first time I arrived home and found Joe passed out on the wooden floor, I called 911. I dragged him into the shower where the well water ran ice cold. The medics responded, revived him with Narcan. When he came to, he gave me a foolish grin and then vomited all over the kitchen linoleum. "Oops," he said. The troopers warned him. "You can't count on us getting here in time." He put an arm around them. "Don't worry about me," he said. They looked at him like he was a lost cause.

Emile had his own troubles. Robert had informed him they had exhausted their bank loan. Memorial Day came and went, but the dinner traffic did not pick up. The days were still gray, evenings chilly.

"By the Fourth of July, the summer crowds will arrive," I reassured them. "The berry crops will ripen."

Despite his resolve, Joe let the peonies get leggy. The first blooms fell to the ground where grazing deer trampled them.

Joe overdosed two more times. The medics arrived, each time with less urgency.

The third time, I stayed in the kitchen while they administered the Narcan. A well-meaning medic asked me if I attended Al-Anon meetings.

"Addiction is insidious," he said. "You've got to take care of yourself. This disease can bring family members to their knees."

Joe wandered the house in his underpants. He stopped apologizing.

The night Emile told me Robert and he were selling the restaurant and returning to New York, I stayed late. "The prices we would have to charge to break even are unsustainable," they explained. "We need to cut our losses."

We split a bottle of cabernet and sat in the empty dining room. The sun hung in until after nine and the thrushes' song echoed through the transparent green of unfurled leaves outside the hopeful windows. Vermont was as lovely as any place in the universe. The long winter intensified the glory of summer's arrival; the lush greenery and thickets of wildflowers refused to be tamed.

I drove home with the convertible top down, alert for deer jumping across the road. In the city, you never saw a moon or stars shine so brightly. I kept thinking of that phrase: "cut our losses."

Arriving home, I switched off the car's engine and sat down on the porch swing. Overnight, the peonies had sprung to life. Large gaudy blooms topped their fragile stems. I knew they would succumb to the torrential rain of the next thunderstorm, but that night they filled the night air with a strident fragrance. I inhaled their bravery and then walked over to the shed for my pruning shears. One by one, I cut off their heads. I filled a bucket with water from the spigot and arranged the flowers in the bucket, allowing each to stand tall. As I assembled my arrangement, I listened for signs of life, for the Morse code of footsteps inside the house, but heard only the barred owl's familiar cry: "Who cooks for you? Who cooks for you?"

Carrying the flowers like a shield, I walked into the house.

# MAC'S STORY

My landlord is threatening to bulldoze my cabin. "You're six months behind in the rent." For thirty-five years, he's tried to get me off his land. Last winter, he turned off my electricity, but I got by with the wood stove. I almost lost my blackberries when the refrigerator died. Instead, I put a pot on the stove and boiled up a humongous vat of jam. On Christmas Eve, I put on my Santa suit and went from house to house, knee deep in snow, giving out sticky jars as gifts. Most of my neighbors, second homeowners from Connecticut or New Jersey, invited me in for a glass of Christmas cheer. "Thirsty," I said and raised my empty for a refill. Some offered Christmas cookies, which I declined. When the refills dried up, I continued my way around the block.

My Boston Brahmin accent opens doors every time. The second homeowners figure I come from something better, that my life in a flea-infested two-room log cabin is an eccentric choice which I can abandon at will. I reassure them that the next job is just over the horizon, that by January I will build log cabins in Haiti. Or that a rich investor in upstate New York has already put down his deposit. I point to the large vacation home on the hill that I built ten years ago, my crew of Slovakian green-carders stranded for the winter after I ran out of cash. Never mind that the owner still complains about the unfinished work. The stone chimney is a work of art. The usual problem, leveraging a new job to complete the old, catches up with me sometimes. Not that the neighbors understand, with their perpetual renovations of houses that sit empty more than they are lived in. When I asked to crash in their empty homes, just to get by for the winter, they banded together to keep an eye out for uninvited squatters.

So now, most of my belongings are in a storage bin deposited on the lot of an abandoned house, hidden behind overgrown vegetation. I've received my third eviction notice. Tim, who drank with me before his wife gave him an ultimatum, promised me he would keep an eye out for their safety.

I remain optimistic. I place an ad in the local paper: Log Homes, forty years of national and international projects. The key is the "national and international." I am better off when my reputation does not precede me. My French is impeccable, my Spanish passable. One job, preferably somewhere warm, and I'll make it through the winter. The Abenaki, even when they were at war, suspended battle for the depth of the season. In Vermont, you do what you have to do to get by.

I tie Harpo and Marx to the porch railing. I prefer to let my dogs run free, but the animal control lady threatened to take them away.

I park my car, which I purchased for $500 during a somewhat blurry night of tequila shots at the Silo, in front of my ill-fated cabin. I only use it for emergencies. In the trunk, there is a can with just enough gas to get into town. I prefer to walk to the bottom of the hill. From the post office, I can hitch rides from neighbors checking their PO boxes. I seldom have to wait long before someone stops and offers me their backseat in exchange for the lowdown on the progression of the local realtor's brain tumor, the most recent string of break-ins, or to ask why my landlord removed my illegal electrical hook up, installed by a buddy when the power was cut.

Sometimes, just to reassure the nervous neighbors, I allude to family, to homes on the North Shore and the Cape. I reference a brother, careful never to give traceable details. That is the agreement. Never embarrass relatives and, in exchange, from time to time they come to my rescue. For example, a cousin settled the account at the Retreat last year when I needed to clean up. Mom's will specified that I should never have direct access to the limited funds left in my name. My brother, who takes the family's legacy seriously, made it very clear that I am better off dead, and most of my relatives agree.

A month after the funeral in a meticulously landscaped cemetery on the Cape, I visited my mom's grave. But even her tombstone reminded me I did not belong there, despite having worn a clean, not inexpensive, shirt borrowed from a man with whom I had spent the night. Mom always reminded me that our family's life was on public display. She treated me like a carefully guarded embarrassment, stashing me away at prestigious boarding schools during my rebellious high school years.

By my freshman year at university, I had the brilliant idea that I would end it all with a glorious run down the highest trail on the back side of Mt. Snow. A cataclysmic collision with a towering maple would save my mom, by then a grieving widow, any further cause for embarrassment. Having downed half a dozen shots of Mt. Snow's finest, I was strapping on my ski boots in the moose-festooned lodge when I looked up and encountered Teddy's gray-flecked eyes appraising my possibilities. The best idea I ever had flew right out of that snow encrusted window.

Teddy saw me, a lonely college guy with what he later called my "Fuck 'em all, life's a party" smirk, and he smirked right back.

"Just call me Mac," I told him. He had money. A founding partner in one of the early computer companies, he had cashed out at just the right time.

I told Teddy that my parents were well-meaning socialists with a religious bent but had died in a car crash, leaving me a small inheritance. Over beers in the lounge, I confessed to dreams of skiing in the Olympics squashed by chronic injuries, a trick knee, a suspicion of an auto-immune disorder. I bragged about an internship with the "cement king" of the North Shore.

Teddy laughed it all off. He couldn't care less who I was, as long as we were high, and the sex was good. He was one hell of a skier. We couldn't get enough. By the time April arrived and even the most expensive snow-making equipment couldn't lay down enough white stuff to coat the runs, we were an item. That summer, Teddy taught me how to build. He had this thing for honest trade. Together we built a house from scratch, starting with pines we felled ourselves and completing our project by choosing perfect stones from the brook for the facing on the chimney.

"Listen up, ladies," the drunks at the local bar proclaimed. "If a man doesn't know how to hunt or fish, he might as well be your girlfriend." The locals did not hesitate to speak their minds. If the liquor flowed, we never took them on. They were hunters. They had guns.

Teddy died of a heart attack in our bed on a Memorial Day weekend. I called Jessie, the local constable. Jessie was a former rock-and-roll guitarist who once played with Springsteen before flaming out on drugs and booze. He moved to Vermont to escape the craziness. Now he is righteously sober with poorly fitting dentures. He pops them in and out of his mouth. He has a wife, five kids, an enormous belly, and a smoker's cough. "What do you want me to do?" he asked me. "He's dead." The usual calamities of a holiday weekend overwhelmed the emergency services. The ambulance didn't arrive to take away Teddy's body for three days. I had plenty of time to ditch our ample supply of coke, but not half enough time to figure out what to do next.

To my surprise, Teddy left the house and all his money to an ex-wife and three children he had never told me about. I had to get out of there, and fast, before my shit came to the attention of the lawyers sniffing around after the death certificate was filed. I packed up what I could. A flyer at the post office advertised a rustic cabin for rent. The simplicity of the two rooms, the anonymity of the ski resort community appealed to me. What the hell, I figured.

I'll stick around for the summer, at least until I get my shit together. This took longer than I anticipated.

During the ski season, I waited tables at the resort in exchange for discount passes. Over the summer, I signed on with a local contractor to build cabins, using the skills Teddy had taught me with such tenderness. The crew, mostly illegal imports from Europe, looked up to me. I spoke to them in their native languages. They bought me beer. On summer evenings, I sat on my front porch listening to Brahms. A woman I met at the general store asked me to watch her puppies, Harpo and Marx, while she visited her old man. She never came back for them.

Word of mouth came in handy. Jessie, besides his job as constable, plowed driveways in the winter and worked as a maintenance man at Stratton in the summer. In between, he took gigs as a self-employed carpenter. Eyeing his customers' driveways, he'd say, "I'd be worried about that crack in the wall if I were you." Once he got the job, he'd brag, "I don't let 'em jew me down, just cut corners wherever I can. Hell, what they don't know can't hurt them." He underbid his jobs and usually shorted the local help he recruited to do most of the work, But the jobs he passed on to me paid enough that I was set for a year. Go figure. I put a lot of love into that pine wainscoting. A load of firewood, a supply of vodka, and a young man just out of prison who needed a place to crash. Over the years, I learned to get by.

Until the bulldozer arrived. My plan now is to go out with a bang.

Just across the border from Brattleboro, there is a desolate stretch of New Hampshire highway dotted with large department stores. Their entire inventory consists of fireworks. Family-owned factory outlets open year round. Display windows plastered with posters advertising Black Cat, Boomer, Magnus, World Class Cowboys. A museum showcase with samples of consumer fireworks manufactured over the past century. The stores advertise video stations for viewing merchandise before selecting the most bang for your buck.

In the summer, Jessie, an avid golfer, plays at a course in New Hampshire. Regardless of how many carpentry jobs he has, he golfs any day the sun comes out. Since he doesn't work when it rains, his customers often complain about the slow pace of their projects. But when I ask him for a ride, he agrees to give me a ride to New Hampshire in his battered black truck.

All the way to Brattleboro, Jessie complains. His clients are demanding. His legs are killing him. This country is going to the dogs, what with Obamacare and fags getting married. Jessie quit smoking the previous summer, and despite the unlit cigar hanging from his mouth, he'd put on fifty pounds and is miserable.

I commiserate, telling Jessie I am expecting a job to come through any day now. A whole new market is opening in Cuba, and just yesterday I received a call inquiring about log cabins for an eco-resort. As he drives, I mull over possibilities, aerial shells containing burst charges and internal time fuses, barrages of rapidly firing explosives, batteries of mortar and bundles of roman candles. Gunpowder in all its glory, chemically altered to burst into color as it explodes in the night sky.

Jessie drops me off on the highway just outside of Brattleboro, still grumbling as his truck drives off in a cloud of exhaust. I walk into the biggest and brightest of the outlets and stand in front of a video showing the World Class Rover, the best-selling 500 Gram Aerial, modeled after the actual rovers that landed on the Moon and Mars. Watching explosion after explosion, I think about the bulldozer on its way to my cabin. I have visions of destroying the machine in a fiery display. Of my humble home lit from within, flames licking the weathered logs. My fellow shoppers buy explosives by the case as the video loop shoots dazzling fire-fueled flowers at the Moon, audio booms ricocheting against ceiling tiles that barely contain the noise. After so many years in the mountains, I have almost forgotten the anticipation of the inevitable explosion, danger laced with promise. In the end, I choose the World Class One Bad Mother. Alternating gold willow, multi-blooming crackling flowers with a final four shot.

When Jessie doesn't show for my return ride, I gather up my merchandise and stick out my thumb. A trucker takes me as far as Brattleboro, where we share a six-pack of beer. A yoga teacher drives me over Hogback Mountain and asks my advice on how to handle her young son, who hates life in the country. In Wilmington, I step into the Pub for another beer, placing my bag of fireworks at my feet as I take my usual barstool. When I complain about being abandoned in New Hampshire, Corey the bartender looks up. Haven't I heard? The place buzzes with the latest gossip. A medivac helicopter flew Jessie to Dartmouth-Hitchcock Hospital after he collapsed on the golf course. The constable had a heart attack or DVTs; at best, he was going to lose his leg. His wife and children were rushing to his side as we spoke. The doctors didn't know if he was going to make it. In all the excitement, no one notices the bag at my feet.

I never had the chance to grieve for Teddy. Our isolation gave us a kind of invisibility. But for Jessie, I put on one hell of a show. Twenty drunks leave that bar to stand on the side of the Deerfield River and watch the display. The night is crystal clear, and the World Class One Bad Mother is phenomenal. "For Jessie," we toast, tighter than any family, drunk on our mortality and the random lunacy of who survives and who succumbs to the ever-present threat of extinction.

Jessie never credits Obamacare with his survival. He claims God was looking out for him. By the time he comes home, eighty-five pounds lighter and short one leg, I am out of rehab. Ninety days sober and feeling good. Harpo and Marx, after a winter with Tim, are at my side again.

My cabin is gone. In its place, a flatbed truck deposited a prefab vacation home. The builder cleared the pines for a mountain view, which must have increased the sale price considerably.

I tell my new landlord I have just completed a project in the Caribbean and wear my Haitian Pride tank top as proof. I just need a room, I tell him, until a Cuban eco-resort gets the proper clearances. In the meantime, I'm finishing up Jessie's jobs. He's singing again, this time gospel songs instead of rock and roll. He never pays me what he owes me, but whenever his grandchildren plan a birthday party, I bring the fireworks.

# ACKNOWLEDGMENTS

Several of these stories appeared in somewhat different forms in literary journals. **How to share a blackberry patch with a black bear** appeared in *Blue Line* in Spring 2019. **Surfacing** appeared in *Open Thought Vortex* in April 2017. **Under Water** appeared in *Cowboy Jamboree* in Spring 2016. **Mac's Story** appeared in *Blood and Bourbon* in February 2019. Thanks to these editors for publishing my work.

For all those glorious summer days at the Green Mountain Writers Conference, my eternal gratitude, especially to Yvonne Daley who brought us all together.

Cover art by Lew Holzman. Thank you, honey!